In the Swamp by the Light of the Moon

Very best,

[signature] Frann

For my lovely Loredana.

A TEMPLAR BOOK

First published in the UK in 2019 by Templar Publishing,
an imprint of Kings Road Publishing, part of Bonnier Books UK,
The Plaza, 535 King's Road, London, SW10 0SZ
www.templarco.co.uk
www.bonnierbooks.co.uk

Text and illustrations copyright © 2019 by Frann Preston-Gannon
Design copyright © 2019 by Kings Road Publishing Limited

1 3 5 7 9 10 8 6 4 2

ISBN 978-1-78741-386-3

This book was typeset in MrsEaves
The illustrations were created with a mixture of ink,
pencils, paints and digital drawing.

Edited by Katie Haworth
Designed by Genevieve Webster

Printed in China

templar
books

In the Swamp by the Light of the Moon

Frann Preston-Gannon

A little frog sat in the night-time air
in the swamp by the light of the moon.
He sat all alone in the little green pond,
singing his little frog tune.

But all by himself his voice was so quiet
so he stopped and he let out a sigh.
"Singing alone is not much fun,
what a lonely wee froggy am I."

So he hopped and he jumped over lily-pad leaves
and into the blue of the night,
to find someone else to join his song
to make it sound just right.

He found a friendly crocodile,
who was drumming and humming in time.
"My friend," he called, "will you sing with me?
Will you add your song to mine?"

So the crocodile hummed
and beat his drum,
while the little frog sang his tune.

But something was wrong
as they both sang along
in the **swamp**
by the light of the
moon.

They found some mice on a fallen log
who were playing a miniature gong.
Into the night they sang, "LA DE DA!"
and froggy called, "Please sing along."

So the mice sang, "LA!"
to the brightest star,
the crocodile hummed
and beat his drum,
while the little frog sang his tune.

But something was wrong
as they all sang along
in the **swamp**
by the light of the
moon.

Down in the murky depths of the pond,
the fish sang, "OH OH OH!"
So the frog blew a kiss to those little fish
and they added their voice to the flow.

The fish sang, "OH!"
in the pond below.
The mice sang, "LA!"
to the brightest star.
The crocodile hummed
and beat his drum
while the little frog sang his tune.

But something was wrong
as they all sang along
in the **swamp**
by the light of the
moon.

Some birds flew down from high above
when they heard the hullabaloo.
"We love the song you're singing,
and we want to join in too!"

So the birds sang, "COO!"
and the noise just grew.
The fish sang, "OH!"
in the pond below.
The mice sang, "LA!"
to the brightest star.
The crocodile hummed
and beat his drum,
while the little frog sang his tune.

But something was wrong
as they all sang along
in the **swamp**
    by the light of the
       moon.

Froggy put down his small guitar.
The song still wasn't quite right.
But then he saw a shy little bug
not adding her song to the night.

"What's wrong?" he said, "why are you so quiet?
Please join our night-time ditty."
"Not me," said the bug. "I'm far too small,
and my voice just isn't that pretty."

"My friend," said frog, "your song's unique
and important like all of the rest.
Even small voices count, so let's hear yours —
only *you* sing your song best."

So the bug sang out her very own song
and her small voice carried far.
She bizzed and she buzzed to the beat of the swamp
and she lit up the night like a star.

So the birds sang, "COO!"
and the noise just grew.
The fish sang, "OH!"
in the pond below.
The mice sang, "LA!"
to the brightest star.
The crocodile hummed
and beat his drum,
while the little frog sang his tune.

And as the song spread all through the swamp,
each voice blended in with the rest.
Now everyone knew that the song of the swamp
needed everyone's voice to sound best.

Together the animals, plants and the moon,
the earth, the pond and the shining stars too,
they all sang together their wonderful tune
in the swamp by the light of the moon,
the moon . . .

. . . in the swamp
by the light of the
moon.